This book belongs to

· ·

My teddy's name is

· ·

Old Bear
and His Friends

JANE HISSEY

HUTCHINSON
London Sydney Auckland Johannesburg

For Nigel, Gill, Samantha and Sarah

First published in 1988 by
Random House UK Ltd
20 Vauxhall Bridge Road
London SW1V 2SA

Designed by Polly Dawes

ISBN 0 09 185101 7

Printed in Singapore

CONTENTS

BILLY BEAR AND THE PARTY OF SURPRISES

The toys all knew it was Billy Bear's birthday. He'd been telling them for weeks, to give them plenty of warning. Then, on the day, they found a huge notice written on the blackboard in the middle of the room. It said: YOU ARE ALL INVITED TO A PARTY OF SURPRISES – COME AS YOU ARE OR COME IN DISGUISES. The notice also told them that the party was to be that afternoon at the far end of the playroom. Everyone thought a party of surprises sounded very exciting. Billy thought that it was a pity he knew what all the surprises were. He had to, because he'd planned them. But it wouldn't really matter, because everyone was bound to bring him a birthday present and, 'Presents are the best surprises,' he said to himself.

All morning, he worked very hard preparing his

surprise party. He made jellies with whole fruits hidden in the middle. He made some egg, some cheese, and some banana sandwiches, and he made little paper flag-shaped labels to tell people which was which. Then he swapped the flags round. Now the cheese ones were labelled 'banana', and the egg sandwiches said 'cheese'. 'That will surprise the others,' he said. He also made a pretend cake by painting a shoe box to look like one; but he made a real cake, too, so that the toys wouldn't be too disappointed. He made a special banana milk shake for his friends to drink, but he coloured it pink so that people would expect it to taste of strawberries! When he'd put holes in some of the squeaky blowers, so that they didn't quite squeak, and stuck a few paper hats up so you couldn't get your head into them, he decided that, at last, he was ready.

But, as a final touch, he hid all the food and drink around the room. 'It will surprise everyone to see no food at a party,' he said. 'I'll let them discover it.'

The time of the party came at last and everyone marched down to the far end of the playroom. As each toy arrived, Billy was handed a birthday card in an envelope with 'Billy Bear' written on the front. 'Thank you very much,' said Billy, putting them on the table. 'I'll open the cards after . . .' He was going to say, '. . .after I've opened my presents,' but he stopped himself, because he suddenly realized that not one of the toys had brought him a present. Oh dear, what a disappointment. A party without presents.

Billy tried to hide his feelings, but just couldn't enjoy things in quite the same way any more. He didn't say anything; after all you don't *have* to give people presents on their birthday. Perhaps it was silly of him to expect to be given things. He decided to make a special effort. 'Come on, everyone,' he said, 'I'll open my cards at the end of the party. Let's all enjoy ourselves.'

The toys were ready for that. They had looked forward all day to the party. Soon they were playing games and dancing. After a little while,

someone came across a plate of food, and then everyone began a food hunt. It was great fun. Every time they found some food, they put it on the table, and soon the table was full of the delicious party food and Billy said that it was time to eat. And then the real fun began!

The food all looked lovely, but it wasn't long before the toys were discovering Billy's little tricks and surprises. When they asked for a sausage roll, Billy rolled a sausage across their plate and laughed. When anyone wanted a rock bun, they found themselves with a real rock with currants stuck to it, and painted to look like a bun. They discovered the surprise sandwiches, usually only by eating them, and they thought the milk shake most peculiar, 'til they realized that, too, was a trick.

But there were nice surprises, too. Billy had invited a magician to come along and do some magic for the toys. His surprises were very clever.

He made bunches of flowers pop out of magic boxes, and handkerchiefs appear from nowhere. At one point, he even made one of Rabbit's friends pop up out of a hat. The toys were delighted; Billy enjoyed it, too. But it didn't quite take his mind off the thought that he hadn't had a single birthday present that day.

At last, the end of the party was drawing near; the food had all gone, except the rock buns, and they'd played as many games with surprise endings as they could think of. Billy wasn't looking quite as happy as he should have been and all the toys knew why.

'Why don't you open your cards, now,' said Old Bear, at last.

'Yes, I should do, shouldn't I,' said Billy. He returned to the heap of cards on the table and carefully tore open the envelope of the first one. Out fell a birthday card that said, 'To Billy, with love from Rabbit,' on it.

'Thank you, Rabbit,' said Billy Bear.

'There's something else,' said Rabbit, 'look in the envelope.'

Billy peeped inside and saw a piece of paper. He drew it out and read what it said, 'This piece of paper entitles you to one carrot and sultana cake to be baked by me, Rabbit, on the day of your choice.'

'Oh Rabbit,' said Billy, 'what a lovely idea! I shall look forward to that. Will you make it when my friends come to stay next week?'

'Of course,' said Rabbit. 'It's your present. You can have it whenever you like.'

'Thank you very much,' said Billy, 'it's a wonderful present.'

Billy returned to his cards and opened the next one. It was from Old Bear and there was a piece of paper in that one, too. It said that Old Bear would pack Billy a picnic on the first sunny day of the summer. Billy was thrilled. He opened one card after another and, in each, there was a paper promise. Bramwell Brown promised to pick Billy a big bunch of flowers whenever he wanted one; Sailor said he'd teach him to dance the 'sailors' hornpipe' if he needed cheering up; Little Bear said he'd make him a pair of trousers like his own, and Duck said that he would make him a nest whenever he wanted somewhere cosy to sleep.

There were lots more promises from all the toys. Billy was soon promised anything he could have wished for.

'Oh, thank you everyone,' said Billy, 'this has been the best surprise of the day. They're lovely birthday presents and they will last me all year; right up until the next birthday. But now I'm so tired that, Duck, do you think I could have your birthday present tonight? I would just love to curl up in a nice cosy nest and dream about all today's surprises.'

TEDDY NO-NOSE AND THE BLACK BUTTON

Teddy No-nose hadn't actually had a nose for years. He'd lost it when he was a fairly new bear and he'd managed perfectly well without one. There weren't many things he had to smell, and the other toys were so used to seeing him without a nose that they hardly teased him at all. In fact, some of the newer toys thought that Teddy No-nose had *never* had a nose.

One day, however, Teddy No-nose was watching some of the other toys being packed into a basket. They were going out for the day with the children, and he suddenly realized something: people always played with him at home, as much as with the other toys, but he couldn't remember ever being taken out for the day or away on holiday.

'It must be because of my nose,' he said to himself. 'They're too ashamed of me to take me out in case their friends laugh at me. Perhaps it's time I tried to get a new nose. But where do I find one?'

Teddy No-nose went off in search of Old Bear and asked him where he could get a new nose.

'That's easy,' said Old Bear. 'Take some money from your money box and go to the Teddy Bear Repair Shop. They sell noses there and you'll be able to choose any nose you like.'

Teddy No-nose was quite excited at the idea of choosing a new nose, until he realized that he had no money in his money box. The last time he'd looked, there had just been a button in there. 'Well,' he said, 'I shall just have to earn some money to buy a nose.'

He went off straight away to ask all the toys whether they needed any jobs doing. Within a few minutes, he was busy tidying up the dolls' house.

'We'll give you five pence when you've done it,' said the dolls'-house dolls. Teddy No-nose worked very hard and soon the little house was spotless. The floors and walls were gleaming and the furniture was all in place. 'That's lovely,' said the dolls'-house dolls. 'You've worked very hard and here's your five pence.'

With the precious money in his paw, Teddy No-nose began his next job. Duck had said he would pay him five pence too, if he would help him to find a missing piece of jigsaw puzzle that he'd been looking for for days. Teddy No-nose searched everywhere, lifting things that were too heavy for Duck to lift, and suddenly, there, under a very big book, was the missing piece of jigsaw.

'Wonderful,' said Duck, giving Teddy No-nose a five-pence piece. 'Now you've got two five-pence pieces; that's ten pence altogether. I should think you could buy a new nose for ten pence.'

Teddy No-nose thanked him very much and set off with his ten pence. But he only got as far as the stairs. With one coin in each paw, he'd nothing to hold on with and was trying to go down the stairs just a bit too fast. He slipped, grabbed at the stair carpet, and dropped both the coins. Helplessly, he watched as they bounced down the stairs and disappeared between the cracks in the floor boards. 'Oh no!' he cried, and sat down on the stairs with his head on his paws. 'Now I'll never have a new nose.'

'Why not?' said a voice very near him.

Looking up, he saw Monkey standing beside him. 'Well, I was going to buy a nose,' explained Teddy No-nose, 'and I earned ten pence by working very hard, but now I've dropped it, and that means all I've got in my money box is a button.'

'Well, what's wrong with a button?' asked Monkey.

'There's nothing *wrong* with a button,' said Teddy No-nose, 'but it won't buy me a new nose, will it?'

'No,' said Monkey, 'but what colour is it?'

'I can't remember,' said Teddy No-nose. 'I'll have a look.'

Fetching his money box, he undid the little cork at the bottom. Out dropped a shiny, round, black button. 'What does the button remind you of?' said Monkey.

Teddy No-nose stared at the button and then he stared at Monkey. And then he realized that Monkey's nose and eyes were all made from buttons. 'Of course,' he said, picking up the button. 'It looks like a nose.'

'That's right,' said Monkey. 'You don't need to buy a nose because you've already got one; a button nose.'

Teddy No-nose was very

excited and could hardly stand still long enough for Monkey to sew on his new button nose. It looked very smart – better than any shop-bought one.

The children still didn't take him out, though. 'It wasn't because of your nose,' they explained, 'you're just too big to fit in the basket.'

But he didn't mind staying at home now, because he had a new friend; a friend with a button nose just like his.

And Monkey and Teddy No-nose spend many hours sitting together, trying to think of a name for a teddy who used to have no nose, but who now has a button. They haven't thought of one, yet; I wonder whether they ever will.

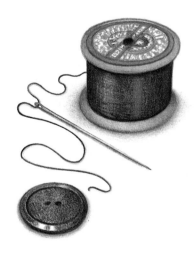

THE BEDTIME PONY

He doesn't do much in the daytime
And I can't take him outside,
Though he's a sort of pony
He's too small for me to ride,
His stuffing's rather lumpy
In his hooves and in his head,
But he's always waiting for me
When I snuggle up in bed.

He's not the sort of pony
Who can walk or pull a cart,
And no one dares to wash him
Just in case he falls apart,
His coat is rather faded
(All the pink bits should be red)
But he's always there beside me
When I'm sleeping in my bed.

DUNCAN BARKER AND THE TARTAN RUG

The toys were all a little worried when Duncan Barker came to live with them. The first thing he did was to chase Rabbit round and round the room. 'I always chased rabbits in Scotland,' he explained.

'I'm afraid I can't live here with that new dog,' puffed Rabbit, out of breath from running. 'I shall never have any peace.'

'Don't worry, Rabbit,' said Snowy the old white bear. 'He tried to get me to wear a kilt, this morning, but I expect he'll settle down soon.'

But Duncan Barker didn't settle down. The next day he upset the dolls'-house dolls by cooking porridge on their cooker and not washing up the saucepan. 'I always cook porridge for breakfast,' he explained.

'We can't live with that new dog,' said the dolls'-house dolls, 'we'll never have any clean saucepans.'

'It's all right, he's just getting used to things, I

expect,' said Snowy.

But things got worse. The following morning
the toys were woken to a dreadful, squeaking,
whining noise. It was Duncan Barker, of course.
He'd tried to make bagpipes out of a hot-water
bottle and it hadn't worked very well. 'I always
play the bagpipes first thing in the morning,' he
explained.

'Oh no,' groaned the other toys.

Well, a few days after that, there was an
enormous commotion at bedtime. 'Ow!' yelled
Bramwell Brown. 'There's something prickly down
my bed!'

'Ooh!' quacked Duck. 'It's got me too.'

'Duncan Barker,' shouted Snowy, 'what have
you done this time?'

'Oh,' said Duncan,
'I think you've found my

27

thistle collection. I always collect thistles.'

'Thistles!' chorused the other toys. 'Why thistles?'

'Because thistles remind me of my real home,' said Duncan Barker.

'And where is your real home?' asked Snowy.

'In Scotland, of course,' replied Duncan Barker.

'Well, I wish you could go back there,' said Bramwell Brown, picking prickles out of his paws.

'So do I,' said Duncan. And, miserably, he left the room to practise his bagpipes in the bathroom.

'Bramwell Brown, that wasn't a very kind thing to say,' said Snowy. 'If Duncan is missing his home, then we must make him feel at home here. If he were happier, then he probably wouldn't be so much trouble. Let's look for things that will make him feel more at home.'

While Duncan Barker was out of the room, the toys rushed about getting things ready for his return. They found a lovely tartan rug in the blanket box and put it in a cosy corner of the playroom. Then they put Duncan's thistle collection with it and a special bowl for him to have his porridge in. Bramwell Brown,

who was good at painting, painted a lovely picture of mountains and valleys and pinned it up near the tartan rug. 'There,' he said, 'I'm sure Duncan will like that.'

And of course, he did. 'Oh it's just like home,' he barked, running round and round the tartan rug. 'Everyone has tartan rugs in Scotland – and what a lovely porridge bowl. Can I make you all a nice bowl of porridge?'

'Thank you very much,' said Snowy, 'we'd like that.'

And while Duncan made them all some porridge, Snowy talked to him about Scotland.

Duncan Barker felt quite at home after that. He went to Scotland sometimes for his holidays, but the rest of the time, he lived in the little Scottish corner of the playroom and was almost no trouble at all. He never quite mastered the hot-water bottle bagpipes, though, however hard he tried.

THE JUMBLE SALE

Little Bear burst into the playroom in a terrible fluster. He upset a jar of marbles and tripped over a jigsaw that had taken Rabbit all morning to do. 'Quick, everyone!' he called, rolling across the room on the marbles. 'It's an emergency!'

'What is it, Little Bear?' asked Rabbit, crossly. 'What on earth's happened?'

Little Bear led Rabbit out into the garden and there, pinned to a tree, was the terrible sign. It said: JUMBLE SALE ON SATURDAY AT 2 O'CLOCK – JUMBLE WANTED URGENTLY.

'Oh, no,' groaned Rabbit, 'not again. We'll all be sorted out. Quick, let's get back and warn the others. Old Bear's ear has nearly fallen off and Bramwell's got a loose eye.'

They rushed back and warned the other toys and, within five minutes, there was a queue forming at Sarah Elizabeth's cupboard. Now Sarah Elizabeth was a very kind little bear; she was always mending the other toys and making new clothes for them. But today, she looked at the queue of toys waiting for repairs or new clothes, and she knew she couldn't cope. 'No,' she said, 'it's no good, I can't possibly do all this sewing and there's only one answer. If you are to be looking your best by Saturday, I shall have to teach you all to sew so you can do your own repairs and make yourselves new clothes.'

So Sarah Elizabeth made her own little sign. It said: SEWING LESSONS FOR EVERYONE THIS AFTERNOON – MATERIALS PROVIDED – SMARTEN UP OR YOU MAY BE SENT TO THE JUMBLE SALE.

By the time Sarah Elizabeth had had her lunch, all the toys were gathered, eagerly awaiting their sewing lesson.

'Oh do show us how to sew. We don't want to be given to the jumble sale,' said Sylvester Bear. 'My trousers are full of holes. I must have a new pair.'

Sarah Elizabeth emptied out a heap of materials from her rag bag and gave each toy a needle and some thread. All afternoon, she showed them how to make jackets and trousers, bow ties and ribbons. She showed them how to darn noses and mend ears, how to sew on eyes and patch threadbare paws. The toys all listened carefully and worked

very hard. None of them wanted to go to the jumble sale. 'Well done,' said Sarah Elizabeth, when Bramwell mended Old Bear's ear and Old Bear repaired Bramwell's nose. The bears looked very pleased.

Sylvester needed trousers and, sorting through the rag bag, he found some tartan material that he decided would really suit him. Sarah Elizabeth helped him to cut out the shapes he needed and then he sewed them together himself. His trousers looked wonderful. Then everyone wanted trousers.

Rabbit and his cousin Reggie made themselves whole sets of clothes. 'Nobody will give us to a jumble sale,' said Rabbit, 'we look like new toys.' It was true, they all looked brand new. Their ears were fixed on firmly, their paws didn't have any holes and their eyes weren't hanging on by a thread.

Sarah Elizabeth was very pleased with everyone, especially Rabbit, who looked extremely smart. 'You're all really clever,' she said. 'I don't think I shall need to sew for you any more.'

The next day, the day of the jumble sale, the whole family came into the playroom to look for toys that could be given away. 'I'm sure there are some that have noses or ears missing,' said the children's mother. 'Let's have a look.'

They walked round the room and found a row of toys sitting there, smart, clean, well dressed and without a single wobbly nose or ear between them.

'It does seem strange,' said the children's mother a few minutes later as she walked out of the room, 'I never realized what good condition the toys were all in. I thought I'd find lots to give away to the jumble sale, but all I could find were these,' and she held up a bag of marbles and a jigsaw puzzle. 'Perhaps we'll find some broken toys for the next jumble sale,' she said.

But now that all the toys could sew they never allowed themselves to get threadbare again. And as a very special thank you to Sarah Elizabeth, they all made her a beautiful new dress. 'We want you to have this,' they said, 'because you saved us from being given away, and now we never

need to worry about notices pinned to trees, again.'

And, just for fun, they played jumble sales themselves, using all the old threadbare clothes as jumble. 'We won't have toys at our jumble sale,' they said. 'You can never be sure they are going to good homes and we wouldn't want to worry them.'

FREDDIE AND THE BLACKBERRIES

It was a muddy, misty autumn day and Freddie the teddy decided it was just the day for a walk. He went to the cupboard to fetch his boots and there he found something which didn't belong to anyone in his house. It was an umbrella, but it wasn't just any umbrella, it was a bright red one with a teddy-bear handle carved out of wood. 'Oh dear,' said Freddie, 'I know who that belongs to and I shall have to return it straight away.'

The umbrella belonged to a teddy-bear friend of Freddy's, Alexander Bear, who lived just across the field with another family of children. He'd been to visit Freddy the day before and had forgotten to take the umbrella home.

'Well, it makes a good excuse for a walk,' said Freddie, picking up the umbrella and putting on his boots. 'I shall go and see Alexander straight away.'

Singing happily to himself, Freddie set off down the garden and through the hedge into the field. The field itself was very muddy and Freddie found that the only way to go was round the edge where the ground had not been ploughed up by the tractor. Then he noticed something he'd forgotten all about since last year: blackberries! Big, bright, black, juicy blackberries, hanging there, just waiting to be picked. Oh, I'm sure Alexander Bear would love some of those, thought Freddie. We could have them for tea! And he started to pick pawfuls of the juicy fruit. Soon, he couldn't hold any more.

'I really need something to put them in,' he said, 'but what can I use? I didn't think to bring a basket with me.' And then he remembered the umbrella – Alexander's umbrella. 'Of course,' he said, 'if I open up the umbrella and hold it upside down, I can fill it with blackberries.'

And so he did. He picked and picked until the umbrella was full of the best and most delicious blackberries. Then, as it looked as though it might rain soon, he hurried off along the path towards Alexander's house.

The path was muddy, but Freddie had his boots on so his feet stayed dry. When he was nearly there, the grey clouds could hold on to the rain no longer, and big drops started to patter on to Freddie's head. That's all right, thought Freddie, I've got Alexander's umbrella to keep me dry.

Jane Hissey

And, without thinking, he lifted the umbrella up above his head.

For a moment, Freddie thought that it was raining blackberries, and then he realized his dreadful mistake. When he'd lifted up the umbrella, all the lovely berries had fallen out, bounced off his head, and landed on the path. Miserably, Freddie watched as they sank into the thick, brown mud and disappeared forever. 'Oh no!' he said out loud. 'Now we won't be having blackberries for tea after all.'

Sadly, he walked on to Alexander's house and knocked on the door. The little bear was delighted to see him and was really pleased to have his umbrella back. 'Thank you, Freddie,' he said, 'that was so kind of you. Now come and see what I've been doing.'

And he led his friend through to the kitchen. A wonderful smell met Freddie's nose as he walked into the room. There, amidst the pots and pans, was a row of gleaming jars of jam. 'It's blackberry and apple,' said Alexander proudly. 'There's a jar for you and some for our tea and there are enough blackberries and apples left for us to make a pie.'

Freddie laughed, and told Alexander all about his blackberry picking, and how they'd all fallen out of the umbrella. 'Perhaps it's just as well I

didn't bring you any,' he said, smiling. 'I don't think you could have managed more. You'd have run out of jam jars!'

And the two friends sat down to enjoy their tea.

PETER AND THE PUMPKIN BEAR

Peter Bear sat in his usual place on the windowsill, looking out at the people walking by. Everyone knew Peter was there and every now and then someone would come close to the window and talk to him through the glass. Peter loved all the attention. He would stay there for most of the day and was never lonely for a minute.

Today was a special day. It was the last day in October; Hallowe'en, and lots of people stopped to tell Peter about their exciting plans for parties that night. Before long Peter saw the two children who lived with him coming home from school. They were each carrying a fat, bright, orange pumpkin. Peter thought these might be to eat, but the children had other ideas.

'Look Peter!' they cried, rushing into the house. 'We're going to make faces with these and put candles inside.'

While Peter watched with excitement, they carefully cut off the top of one of the pumpkins, then they began to dig out the middle with a spoon. That looks fun, thought Peter. But when the children cut a face for their pumpkin Peter changed his mind. He could hardly bear to look – the horrible, cross, monster face had staring eyes and gappy teeth in a wicked sort of grin. The children were delighted, but Peter put his paws over his eyes. With the help of their parents, the children put a candle inside the pumpkin head and lit it. Straight away the pumpkin face shone with a fiery, red glow. It looked even more frightening now and seemed to stare at Peter. When the children put it on the windowsill it glared out at the people walking by and nobody dared to come near the window.

When everyone had left the room, Peter peeped out from behind his paws. 'What can I do?' he said. 'With that thing there frightening everyone, nobody will come over to talk to me.' He crept over to blow out the candle, but thought the children would be cross with him if he did that. And then he saw the other, unused pumpkin and an idea came to him. Using the knife and spoon the children had used, he cut the top off the spare pumpkin and hollowed out the middle. Then he began to cut a face in his pumpkin, but his pumpkin face was a happy, friendly face. In fact it was the face of a smiling teddy bear. Peter carried

the finished pumpkin to the windowsill and put it down carefully beside the monster face. Then, as he knew he shouldn't use a candle in case he burnt his paws, he fetched a torch to put inside his pumpkin bear. Straight away it smiled out with a warm, orange glow and the people walking by were so surprised to see a friendly bear face that they came over to take a closer look. All Peter's friends arrived to talk to him about his pumpkin and they took no notice of the monster face at all.

In fact so many people liked Peter's idea that they all made pumpkin bears too. And it turned out to be the most unfrightening Hallowe'en anyone had ever known.

THE CHRISTMAS FANCY DRESS PARTY

The Christmas holiday seemed to be a time for the new toys. All the old ones found themselves sitting upstairs with nobody to play with. 'It's not very exciting, is it?' said Mo, the mohair bear, as he paced up and down the playroom.

'Well, we could do something exciting,' said Old Bear. 'Let's have a fancy dress competition, a Christmas one.'

'That's a good idea,' said Rosie and Fluff, two very small bears. 'We know what we could dress up as.' Whispering and laughing, they rushed off into a corner to plan their costumes.

Soon all the toys were busy finding, making, or trying on their fancy dress costumes. They were all very excited. 'I'm going to dress up as a king,' said Mo. 'I can just imagine myself in a beautiful crown.'

'Where will you get a crown?' asked Little Bear.

'I shall pull a cracker,' said Mo. 'They always have paper crowns inside.'

Old Bear and Little Bear settled themselves down in a chair to judge the competition. Rosie and Fluff had left the room to fetch something. 'They said they wouldn't be long,' said Old Bear. 'When they come back we'll start the judging.' Looking round the room he didn't recognize any of his friends any more, they were all in disguise. 'They do look good costumes,' he said. 'It's going to be very hard to judge the best.'

Everyone was eager to get started and still Rosie and Fluff weren't back. 'I think we'd better begin without them,' said Little Bear. 'They might be ages.'

Bramwell Brown was the first to be judged. He had rolled himself up in a piece of paper and was lying on the floor. 'What are you meant to be?' asked Old Bear.

'Bang!' said Bramwell Brown.

'I think it's an exploding sausage,' said Little Bear.

'BANG!' said Bramwell Brown even louder.

'I know,' said Mo, 'it's a Christmas cracker.

'Oh, well done!' said Old Bear. 'I can see it is now. What a clever idea!'

King Mo was next. He marched in front of the judges with his cracker crown on and a king's robe made from a piece of red crêpe paper. He looked very smart indeed and everyone cheered.

The next thing to shuffle in front of the judges seemed to be a walking paper chain. It moved along like a brightly coloured, rustling snake. 'It seems to be a paper chain that can walk,' said Little Bear, 'but I can't see who's under it.'

'It's us, it's us!' cried the little yellow bears, Marigold and Buttercup. 'We knew you'd never see us.' The paper chain suddenly tripped over its paws and ended up a heap of bears and paper. Marigold and Buttercup grinned at the judges from under the heap. 'We're a paper chain that's fallen down now,' said Marigold, 'they do you know, sometimes.'

'Of course they do,' said Old Bear, 'that's very good.'

While everyone was busy clapping the fallen paper chain, in jumped Rabbit. He was covered in white cotton wool and had a carrot tied over his nose.

'Oh look,' cried Little Bear, 'a white rabbit.'

'I'm not a white rabbit,' said Rabbit, crossly, 'that wouldn't be Christmasy. I'm a snowman.'

'Well, a snow *rabbit* then,' said Little Bear.

'You've left your ears sticking up. Snowmen don't have long ears.'

Old Bear fetched a woolly hat and, tucking Rabbit's ears inside it, popped it over the snow-rabbit's head. 'There,' he said, 'you look wonderful now, Rabbit.'

While the toys were admiring Rabbit, the door opened and something prickly came in. 'What is it?' said King Mo. 'It looks like a holly bush.' But when they looked closer, the toys could see that inside the bush were two pairs of eyes.

'It's Rosie and Fluff!' said Old Bear. 'But what are you supposed to be?'

'We're holly bears,' said Rosie, proudly.

'What are holly bears?' asked Rabbit, not sure whether he should know.

'Oh, you know,' said Fluff. 'There's a Christmas song called "The Holly and the Ivy" and it's got a bit in it all about holly bears. I don't know what they look like, but they must be something like this.' And with that, the whole holly-covered pair of bears did a little twirl to show off its disguise.

'Well, if holly bears look like a bush, then you've done very well,' said Old Bear.

When everyone had clapped the holly bears, Old Bear and Little Bear discussed the winners.

'We really think,' said Old Bear 'that you've all done so well, you should all win something, but what can the prize be?'

'A crown!' shouted Rosie. 'In the Holly Bears' song it says something like, "the holly bears the crown".'

'Oh, I remember,' said King Mo, 'and I know how we can all have a prize *and* a crown.'

'How?' asked the others.

'Crackers,' said Mo.

On the table in the room had been a whole box of crackers. Mo had only used one to get the crown for his king costume. It had been a box of ten crackers and there were nine left. And so they all won prizes for their costumes and they all felt very much jollier in their paper party hats. There were even enough crackers for the judges to have one each and they did deserve them, didn't they?

SPOTTY BEN

Ben saw his own reflection
In the mirror on the wall.
'I seem to be all spotty;
I can't be well at all.'
'It's all right,' laughed the other toys,
'None of your spots are new.
You've always had a spotty coat,
That's how we know it's you.'

POLLY AND THE WARM SNOWMAN

There had not been a single flake of snow all winter. Almost every morning the toys had crowded eagerly on to the windowsill hoping to look out on to a snow-covered garden. Some of the newer toys had never seen snow and they were just beginning to wonder whether perhaps it didn't really exist.

And then one morning there it was; a thick blanket of snow over everything. They woke up and wondered why it was so quiet. There were no footsteps on the path or wheels on the road; even the birds were too busy keeping warm to sing. The toys almost fell off the windowsill, they were so excited.

'We'll build a snowman,' they shouted, and all rushed to the door and tumbled into the garden in a heap.

It was then that they realized just how deep the snow was. Only the tallest teddy bears with the longest legs could actually walk about. Most of the others had disappeared completely. 'Oh dear,' said the muffled voice of Polly, a particularly small bear, 'I can't move at all. The snow is so deep it comes up to my ears.'

The others helped to pull her out and then Freddie the teddy fetched a tea tray from the kitchen. All the smaller toys clambered on to the tray and were towed across the snow-covered lawn by the bigger ones. They walked round and round the garden until they found a place that looked just right for their snowman and then they set to work.

Freddie and the other big bears made a snowball and began to roll it across the garden. As it rolled it picked up more and more snow and left a trail behind it of bare grass just like a wiggly green path. The small bears were very pleased to see this and, leaving their tea-tray sledge, they ran along the green path and helped the big bears push the heavy snowball.

After a while the snowball was large enough to be the body of the snowman.

'We need a head now,' said Polly, and began to pat a snowball into shape with her paws. They rolled this one right round the lawn making a big O-shaped path and arrived back at the snowman's body with a snowball big enough to be his head.

'How are we going to get it up on top of the body?' asked Freddie. 'Even I can't reach.'

But Polly had a plan. 'We've got the tea tray,' she said. 'We'll roll the snowball head on to the tray and pull it up with a rope. It shouldn't be too difficult.'

They all rolled the snowman's head on to the tray and threaded a skipping rope through the handles. Then the strongest bears climbed up to the top of the snowman's body with the ends of the rope and pulled. Slowly the tea tray, with the snowball head on it, rose into the air until it was level with the bears.

'It's up! We've done it,' shouted Freddie, and he rolled the head neatly into place. The toys down below cheered and jumped up and down with excitement.

'He needs a face,' called one little bear. The tea tray was lowered down and some of the toys went off to fetch coal for the snowman's eyes, a carrot for his nose and twigs for his mouth and eyebrows.

Very soon the snowman was smiling down at them with his twiggy mouth and his shining, coal-black eyes. Before Freddie climbed down he took off his own stripy scarf and tied it round the neck of the snowman.

'He looks lovely,' said Polly. 'We'll keep him for ever and ever and come and play with him every day.'

They spent the whole afternoon in the garden – throwing snowballs, making slopes out of snow and sliding down them on the tray. When it began to get dark they said goodnight to the snowman and went indoors to bed.

The next morning the sun was shining brightly and the toys couldn't wait to get outside. But when they opened the door they all stopped and stared. 'Somebody's stolen our snowman,' cried Freddie. It seemed to be true: the lovely snowman had vanished.

Then Polly noticed something lying on the ground. 'But they left behind the carrot nose,' she said.

'And the coal eyes,' added Freddie. 'And my scarf.'

And then they realized what had happened to their snowman. He hadn't been stolen – he'd melted. What's more, the snow had almost gone too. There wasn't enough to build another snowman. Feeling very sad, the toys began to play with the

last of the snow. But the sun was quite warm now and even the last of the snow was melting fast.

Polly had an idea and went indoors again. The others could see her sitting by the window, knitting. She looked up and waved every now and again, but she seemed very busy.

By the end of the day the grass was as green as it was in summer. The only snow left was in the shady bit under the tree. The toys gave up trying to make things with the snow and trooped indoors.

'It's nearly spring now,' said Freddie to Polly, when he found her sitting by the fire. 'I don't think it will snow again this winter, so we won't be able to make another snowman for a whole year.'

'No,' said Polly, 'but I have a surprise for you Freddie,' and she pointed to a corner of the room. In soft white wool with black eyes and a carrot-shaped nose stood a little knitted snowman. He was smiling at Freddie and was wearing a knitted hat and scarf just like Freddie's own.

'He's a warm snowman, Freddie. I knitted him myself. The outdoor snowman may have melted, but this one never will.'

'We can play with him all year,' said Freddie. 'Oh Polly, you are clever!' And holding one white arm each they led the little warm snowman out of the room to show all the other toys.

Of course, he never melted. In fact, he's still there to this day.

MR BROWN AND THE BABY BEAR

Mr and Mrs Brown were teddy bears. They lived in a little cupboard in the playroom. They had furnished the cupboard home themselves with things that Mr Brown had found while out walking. He'd brought back acorns for them to use as cups, and soft feathers that he'd found near the duck pond to stuff cushions with. He'd made mirrors from old milk bottle tops and a broom from twigs that he'd collected. All their tables were made from little boxes.

In fact their cupboard was cluttered with the bits and pieces that he'd collected and one day Mrs Brown decided that it was full enough. 'If you go out today,' she said to Mr Brown, 'then you are not to come back with anything. I shall check that your paws are empty when you walk in that door.'

Mr Brown hugged her as usual and set off out of the cupboard, across the room, down the stairs and out into the garden.

It was a lovely autumn day and a

carpet of leaves covered the lawn. Mr Brown thought it was great fun crunching through the leaves. He found some especially interesting ones which he thought of taking home but, remembering Mrs Brown's warning, he left them where they were. 'It's a pity,' he said. 'I'm sure I could have made something with them.'

A little further down the garden he found a bright, shiny brown conker. 'Oh what a beauty!' he said to himself as he bent down to polish the gleaming nut with his paw. 'The case it came out of must have been huge.' And then he saw it –the biggest, most perfect conker case he'd ever seen. The inside was silken smooth and white and shaped like a round-bottomed bowl. The outside was hard and covered in prickles.

'I'm sure I could put something in it,' said Mr Brown, but he remembered Mrs Brown and sadly left it where it was.

Mr Brown continued down the garden until he came to the fence at the end. He was just about to turn and go back to the house when he saw a heap of leaves. They'd been raked up the day before and piled against the fence.

Mr Brown gazed at the heap and sighed.

There was one thing he'd always wanted to do and that was to jump right into the middle of

a heap of dry, crunchy autumn leaves.

Shall I, he thought to himself. Just to see what it's like – to see whether it's soft or crunchy or bouncy. I must find out.

And, looking round to make sure nobody was watching, he climbed up on the fence above the leaves.

'One, two, three,' he said out loud – and then he jumped. It was wonderful. The leaves were all crispy and they crackled softly as he sank gently down, down, down, into the springy heap.

And then, when he'd stopped sinking into the leaves, Mr Brown heard a sound. Someone, or something, very near him said, 'Ow!'

'Well, that wasn't me,' said Mr Brown. 'I'm not hurt.'

'Well, I am,' said a little muffled voice. 'You're sitting on me.'

Mr Brown jumped to his feet and, pushing his paw deep into the leaves, he pulled out the smallest teddy bear you've ever seen.

'Goodness!' said Mr Brown. 'It's Toby Small. How did you get in there?'

'Somebody took me for a walk and dropped me,' said Toby Small, 'and then I was raked up with the leaves. I've been here all night and I'm cold and hungry.'

'Well, Toby,' said Mr Brown, 'I shall take you back to your house this afternoon, but first I think I'd better take you home to Mrs Brown so you can have the leaves brushed out of your fur.'

So Mr Brown picked up the little bear and carried him back to the house. On the way, he stopped to collect the big conker case that he'd found. He had an idea now how he could use it without making Mrs Brown cross.

Mrs Brown was waiting at the door of the cupboard when he arrived back.

'Now,' she said to Mr Brown when she saw the conker case in his paws, 'take that straight back to the garden. We don't need it.'

'But we do,' said Mr Brown, and he put down the conker case so that Mrs Brown could see inside it. There, lying fast asleep in the soft, smooth, white bed was Toby Small. He was tucked up with sheets made from the brightest autumn leaves and he was smiling happily.

'Oh,' said Mrs Brown softly, 'I see. You couldn't really leave him outside, could you?' And she carried the sleeping bear in his conker cot into the little cupboard house.

When Toby Small had had a sleep and a meal and his fur was brushed free of leaves, Mr and Mrs Brown took him home. And after that he

came to stay with them for his holidays and they
kept the conker case for him to sleep in.

Gradually the cupboard house became more and
more cluttered with things that Mr Brown brought
home from his walks, but Mrs Brown never
complained. 'We must have something for
Toby Small to play with when he
comes to stay,' she would say.
And Mr Brown just smiled.

HAZEL'S NIGHT OUT

Hazel, the little brown donkey, and Edward Bear were the very best of friends. They went everywhere and played everything together. Sometimes Hazel pulled Edward round in a little cart and sometimes Edward would pull the cart and give Hazel a ride just for a change. At night when they were tired they tucked themselves into a little corner of the windowsill behind the curtain. Hazel liked to gaze out of the window and dream that she was sleeping in a field like a real donkey. Edward would tuck the curtain round him, snuggle up to Hazel and dream that he was exactly where he really was, in a nice cosy corner of the playroom with his very best friend.

'Why do you pretend you're outside?' Edward asked Hazel one day. 'You'd be cold and miserable if you really slept in a field.'

'Of course I wouldn't,' said the little donkey. 'I have thick fur to keep me warm.'

'Well, I'm quite happy to stay inside,' said Edward.

They settled down in their usual place that

night, but next morning when Edward woke up, Hazel was nowhere to be seen. Edward sat down to try and remember where he'd last seen his friend. 'Now,' he said to himself, 'was she definitely with me last night?' But he already knew the answer. 'Yes, of course she was, because she was talking about how nice it would be to sleep in a field.' Then, 'Oh no,' he said out loud, 'perhaps Hazel has gone outside.'

Edward rushed to look out of the window. It was pouring with rain. The grass glistened, the trees dripped and the sky looked as grey as old saucepans. Edward looked at the lawn and he looked at the hedge, and then he looked at the field beyond the hedge, and then he saw Hazel. She was standing quite still in the middle of the field staring at the ground.

'She's there!' cried Edward, 'she's outside in the field. I'm going out to get her.'

Lots of the other toys said they would come too and soon a crowd of them, wrapped in coats and under umbrellas was trudging across the lawn.

'Hazel,' called Edward, 'come in! You'll get soaked.'

'I can't,' called Hazel.

'What does she mean, she can't?' said one of the other toys.

'I don't know,' said Edward. 'I'll go and find out.'

Edward made his way across the field until he came to his old friend. 'Hazel,' he said, 'have you been out here all night?'

'Yes,' said Hazel, sadly.

'And are you coming in now?'

'No,' said Hazel.

'Why not?' asked Edward.

'Because I'm so wet that my legs are all heavy with rain and I can't walk,' said Hazel, miserably.

'Oh, I see,' said Edward, and patted his friend gently. Sure enough Hazel's fur was so full of rain water that she felt like a sponge.

'Can't you walk at all?' asked Edward.

'Not at all,' said Hazel. 'My hooves feel as though they are fixed to the ground.'

'Don't worry,' said Edward, 'I think I may have the answer.'

Rushing back to the house, he fetched the little cart that Hazel usually pulled. Then, with some of the other toys, he dragged it across the field to the soggy donkey. With everyone pushing and pulling they heaved Hazel into the back of the cart and trundled her across the field and back to the house. Once inside they tipped her out and everyone set to work to rub her fur dry. At last the poor donkey could move again.

'Real donkeys don't get wet, do they?' said Hazel.

'Not as wet as you,' said Edward, kindly. 'But you're not a real donkey, you're a toy donkey and toys have to stay dry.'

But, to make his friend feel more like a real donkey, Edward cut out a picture of a shiny star and pinned it to the curtain. 'Now you can look up and pretend you're outside,' he said, kindly. 'This way you can sleep under the stars and stay dry.'

'I like that,' said Hazel, gazing at the star. 'I think I shall be happy to sleep indoors now.'

THE DOLLS'-HOUSE CHRISTMAS

Christmas had nearly arrived. The toys all knew this because the children were very busy decorating the house. They were too busy to play and they wouldn't let the toys help with the decorations. 'How can you decorate the Christmas tree?' they said to Little Bear. 'You'd get prickles in your fur. And how could you hang paper chains,' they said to Rabbit. 'You couldn't reach.'

They wouldn't let Old Bear help with the holly or Duck put up the fairy lights. It really wasn't much fun at all for the toys. 'We haven't been able to do anything,' grumbled Little Bear. 'I would have loved to help make the house look Christmasy.'

'They could have saved the low-down jobs for us,' said Rabbit.

'What low-down jobs?' said Old Bear. 'There aren't any really, are there?'

'There's the pot the Christmas tree stands in,' said Little Bear, 'that's low down and it's always decorated.'

They all rushed to the Christmas-tree pot only to find that it had just been wrapped in red crêpe paper and tied with a big green bow. 'Oh well, that's that, then,' said Little Bear. 'Now there's nothing left for us to do.'

It was then that he noticed the dolls' house. Standing in the corner of the playroom, it had been completely forgotten. There were no paper chains in the rooms, no Christmas tree with presents underneath, and no holly over the pictures. It looked just as it did all the rest of the year.

'Why haven't you decorated the house?' Little Bear asked the dolls'-house dolls. 'It doesn't look very festive.'

'We haven't any decorations,' said one of the dolls. 'Nobody really bothers with the dolls' house at Christmas time. They're too busy doing other things.'

'Oh, that's wonderful,' said Little Bear. 'We'll decorate it for you. It's just what we wanted. We can reach into every corner of the dolls' house and we'll make the decorations ourselves.'

The other toys were very excited at Little Bear's

idea and, very soon, they were off in search of suitable decorations.

Old Bear was the first to find something. He arrived at the dolls' house carrying a tiny but perfect Christmas tree. 'I found it in the dustbin – it's a little branch that had broken off the big tree,' he explained, 'but it's just the right size for the dolls' house.'

They planted the tiny tree in a little egg cup with soil packed tightly round its stem to stop it wobbling.

'It needs fairy lights,' said the biggest doll. 'What can we use?'

Rabbit rummaged through the button and beads box until he found what he was looking for: some tiny, coloured, glass beads. He threaded them on a piece of green cotton and wound them in and out of the branches of the tree. When the light caught them, they did look just like fairy lights and the dolls'-house dolls were delighted. They found other beads to hang on the tree as decorations and Little Bear stuck a tiny, gold, sticky-paper star on top.

'Well that's the tree done,'
said Old Bear. 'Now for the
rest of the house.'

Little Bear couldn't find any
holly small enough for the dolls' house so he cut
holly-leaf shapes out of green paper and they used
these to decorate the mirrors and to make a
Christmas holly wreath for the front door.

Rabbit sat and cut up very thin strips of
wrapping paper and all the toys used these to
make dolls' house-sized paper chains. Then, Old
Bear, who could comfortably reach into every
corner of the house, hung the paper chains up so
they criss-crossed all the tiny rooms. The dolls'
house was really looking ready for Christmas now
and the toys all began to feel excited.

'We'll put our presents under the tree now,
shall we?' suggested Rabbit. They had all wrapped
presents up to give each other – little things they'd
made or found. They piled these up in a heap
under the tree.

And, as the finishing touch, one of the dolls
rushed off and returned with all the doll-sized socks

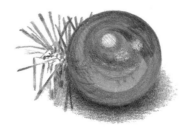

she could find. 'We'll all have to have bare feet until Christmas,' she laughed, 'but we don't mind. There are enough socks here for everyone.' And she hung the socks in a row along the dolls'-house mantelpiece.

'Now the house looks like a real house,' said Little Bear, as he stood back to admire all their work. 'And it has been fun decorating it.'

And do you know, on Christmas morning, when the dolls'-house dolls walked into their sitting room they could hardly believe their eyes, for every tiny sock was full of tiny presents. So they hadn't been forgotten after all, had they?

SUNSHINE SAM AND THE SPECIAL PRESENT

It was Christmas Eve and Sunshine Sam, the yellow bear, sat with the other toys. They were watching the children wrapping each others' presents in bright paper.

'We were all presents once,' said Tom Ted. 'It was lovely, wasn't it? First we were wrapped up in pretty paper and tied round with bright ribbons, then, on Christmas morning, we would feel the ribbon being untied and we would hear excited voices . . . .'

'And then we would jump out and meet all the other toys,' said Sunshine Sam.

'And play with all the games and be hugged and taken out for walks,' said Tom Ted.

'I'd like to be a present again,' said Sunshine Sam. 'It would be lovely to be a surprise for someone.'

'But nobody would be surprised by you now!' said Tom. 'The children would just be disappointed because you aren't new.'

'I'd still like to try,' said Sam.

'Well you can't do it on your own,' said Tom. 'I suppose I'd better help.'

When the children went to bed, Sam and Tom hid behind the curtains. Everyone looked everywhere for them and they nearly came out when they saw how worried the children were at bedtime. 'We wanted them in our beds,' said the little girl, Amy. 'Christmas won't be the same if we can't find Sam and Tom.'

'They'll turn up,' said Mummy and Daddy. 'Don't worry; they can't be far away.'

With their paws tucked up in the curtains, Sam and Tom waited and waited for Mummy and Daddy to go to bed too. Mummy was busy hanging up Christmas cards and Daddy was making paper chains. By the time they'd gone to bed, the two bears had given up waiting and had fallen asleep. It was still dark when they woke up because it was very, very early in the morning.

Tom peeped out from behind the curtain. 'Oh Sam, Father

Christmas has been already,' he said. 'The stockings are all lumpy with presents.'

'Will there still be room for me?' asked Sam.

'Of course there will,' said Tom. 'Come on, it's time to wrap you up.'

The two bears crept over to where the wrapping paper was kept and chose the brightest, prettiest paper they could find.

'Will it fit?' asked Sam. 'I don't want my paws to stick out.'

'It looks fine,' said Tom. 'Come on, we must hurry, it's getting lighter every minute.'

Sam chose the ribbon next – a bright, shiny red one. 'Look, Tom, isn't this lovely,' he said, stroking it with his paw.

'Yes,' said Tom, 'and it is time I was tying you up with it. Hurry now if you want to be a present, the children will soon be down to see what's in their stockings.'

Sam and Tom carefully climbed up to the top of one of the stockings, carrying with them the paper and the lovely red ribbon. Soon they found a little space between a long, thin parcel and a flat, square one.

'Right Sam,' said Tom, 'lie down on the paper and roll yourself up in it.'

Sam stretched out on the wrapping paper and

Tom helped to roll him over and over. It was difficult because they kept bumping into the long thin parcel. Soon, however, Sam began to look more like a present and less like a bear. Now it was time for the ribbon.

'Are you ready?' called Tom.

Sam's muffled voice came through the layers of paper, 'Tie me up, I'll really be a present then.'

Tom folded over the ends of the paper and wrapped the red ribbon around Sam's tummy. Then he tied a lovely bow.

'Have you finished?' called a muffled Sam.

'Yes, you're all ready,' said Tom, tucking the bear-shaped parcel into the top of the stocking. 'See you later, Sam.' He climbed carefully down and settled himself on the sofa to wait for the children. He didn't have long to wait; in less than an hour the children rushed into the room.

'He's been, he's been,' they cried when they saw the bulging stockings. Just look at all the presents.'

They lifted the stockings down and laid them on the sofa. It was then that they saw Tom. 'Tom Ted,' they cried, 'you're here after all. We did so want you to share the fun, but we still haven't found Sunshine Sam – Christmas just won't be the same without him.'

The first parcel to be opened was the long thin one, which had been tucked in next to Sam. 'It's a little umbrella,' cried Amy. 'Oh Sam would have loved this umbrella, he could have gone for walks with me in the rain and kept his fur dry.'

The next present was the flat one on the other side of Sam. 'Oh look,' cried Amy, 'it's a lovely book. I could have snuggled down in bed with Sam to read this but now I can't because he's lost.'

She wiped a tear away and then reached into the stocking for the third parcel. This time it was Sam's parcel. She took hold of it and carefully lifted it out. 'What pretty ribbon,' she said, smiling. 'I wonder what's inside.'

She undid the ribbon and pulled back the wrapping paper. 'Sunshine Sam!' she cried. 'It's you! You aren't lost. But how did you get in there? Perhaps Father Christmas found you and brought you home. Oh I'm so happy! You're the best present I've ever had!'

And she tied the lovely red ribbon round Sam's neck in a big, bright bow, and she showed him her umbrella and her book. 'Come on, Sam,' she said, 'let's open the rest of the presents together.'

'You see, Tom,' said Sam later on, when they were sitting quietly amidst the sea of wrapping paper, 'the children really did like me being a present again. Amy said I was the best one that she has ever had.'

'Yes,' said Tom Ted, 'that's true, but I don't think you'd better try it again. I think being a surprise twice is quite enough.'

THE WINTER PICNIC

Spring had not quite arrived; there were no leaves on the trees or eggs in the nests and all the toys were well wrapped up and sitting around in the playroom.

'Let's go for a picnic,' said Old Bear, suddenly.

'A picnic?' chorused the others. 'But it's cold.'

'Then we'll take warm food and coats,' said Old Bear. 'It's a perfect day for a picnic.'

'Why is it perfect?' asked Bramwell Brown, looking at the trees blowing in the wind outside.

'Because nobody else will be having a picnic,' said Old Bear, 'so we'll be able to choose the best picnic place and have it all to ourselves.'

'And nobody else will be using the picnic basket,' said Little Bear.

'Or the blanket,' added Bramwell Brown.

'That's right,' said Old Bear, getting to his feet.

'Come on, everyone, let's get ready.'

Old Bear filled a hot-water bottle and put it in the bottom of the picnic basket. Then he put everything else in on top. He made the sandwiches with hot toast, and wrapped them up and put them right on top of the hot-water bottle to keep warm. Then he filled a flask with hot soup and wrapped up hot buns, sausage rolls, baked potatoes in their jackets and a jar of honey. He packed a few other bits and pieces while the others fetched blankets, coats and jumpers. Soon they were all ready.

There was just a hint of frost on the path as they marched out of the house, dragging the picnic basket along on a little four-wheeled cart.

'We must be mad!' said Bramwell Brown. 'But it's rather fun to be having the first picnic of the year. Where are we going to have it?'

'I suggest over there,' said Old Bear, pointing to the top of a little hill. 'It will be a nice view up there.'

'It'll be a bit windy,' said Harry Bear, rather doubtfully. 'And we'll have to walk all the way back, don't forget.'

But nobody was really listening; they were pulling and puffing their way up the hill. By the time they were halfway up, most of them had taken off their coats and some had even removed their jumpers. Harry Bear took off his scarf.

'I feel quite warm again now,' said Bramwell, 'and I'm very hungry.'

At last, they reached the highest point. 'This will do,' said Old Bear, spreading out one of the blankets and sitting down in the middle of it. The others joined him. They left the basket on the little path and unloaded the food. The soup in the flask was lovely and warm and they all wrapped their paws around a steaming mug of it. The honey had gone a bit runny and the butter had melted out of the sandwiches, but it all tasted good; in fact, everything tasted especially good and, in no time at all, the food had all gone.

But when they'd finished, the toys began to shiver again. 'Come on,' said Old Bear, 'it's too cold to sit still – let's play some games.'

They played a very quick game of 'hide and seek' and an even quicker game of 'hunt the acorn' and then they rolled pebbles down the hill. Rolling pebbles down the hill wasn't really active enough and, soon, they began to feel chilly again.

'The hot-water bottle is still warm in the picnic basket,' said Bramwell Brown. 'Why don't we all get in with it for a little while, just for a warm up!'

Rubbing their paws together they all climbed into the nearly-empty basket.

'Oh . . lovely,' said Harry Bear, as his paws touched the warm hot-water bottle. 'I'm as warm as summer time, now.'

They all snuggled down while Old Bear told them stories of picnics he used to go on when he was a new bear many years ago. They didn't mind that the basket was a bit sticky with spilt honey, or that there were crumbs all over their fur. 'It's warm in here, isn't it,' said Little Bear. 'I won't want to get out to go home.'

None of them wanted to get out but, as it turned out, they didn't actually have to. They had forgotten that the picnic basket was still on the little four-wheeled cart. Suddenly a big gust of wind caught the open lid and began to blow the basket down the hill. 'Oh no!' cried Old Bear. 'Help!'

But of course there was nobody to help. Nobody else was out having picnics in weather like that. They were the only ones. All they could do was hold on to each other as tightly as they could and hope that the basket wouldn't stop too suddenly.

'It's when things like this happen,' said Bramwell Brown, shakily, 'that you wish you were having a picnic on a normal sort of day when there were lots of people around to rescue you.'

The basket bumped its way on down the little

hill. It jumped a very small stream and headed towards the gate. 'Duck!' shouted Old Bear.

And they all ducked, except Little Bear who was busy *looking* for a duck as they whizzed under the bottom rung of the gate. If anyone had seen the picnic basket now, they would have thought it was just a picnic basket on wheels rolling down the hill. They would never have guessed that there were five brave picnickers inside.

'Oh, when is it going to stop?' asked Little Bear.

'When it gets to the bottom, I should think,' said Bramwell Brown. And he was more or less right. The little cart suddenly hit a log; the basket fell off the cart and the five friends fell out of the basket. When they realized that they weren't moving any more, and dared to look, they found that they were right outside their own front door.

'Well, isn't that wonderful,' said Little Bear, 'a picnic on top of a hill and we didn't even have to walk back.'

'I think perhaps I would rather have walked back,' said Old Bear, standing up rather shakily, 'but for the first picnic of the year, that's going to be hard to beat.'

'Yes,' said Bramwell Brown, 'travelling home from the picnic isn't usually the most exciting bit, is it?'

And gathering up the basket, its contents, and the little cart, they all trooped indoors for tea!

WET BEAR

Barnaby Bear stood on the doorstep feeling cold and damp. What a day to be left out in the rain. How could they have forgotten that he'd been in the garden. It just wasn't fair. He was still standing there gazing out at the rain when Teddy George came into the kitchen. 'Oh dear,' he said. 'What happened to you?'

'I was out in the garden and I fell asleep,' said Barnaby. 'Nobody took me in when it started raining and I'm so wet and cold. How can I get warm and dry?'

'The best thing to do is run around,' said George. 'That always warms you up.'

Barnaby Bear began to run up and down the kitchen. 'Like this?' he puffed, as he passed George for the fifth time. 'Yes, that's the way,' said George. But just as he said it, Dog came through a door and collided with Barnaby. They both landed in a heap. 'Why were you running?' asked Dog. 'To keep warm,' said Barnaby.

'Oh, you'd do better to wrap up in something,' said Dog. Dog and

Teddy George fetched a sheet and wrapped Barnaby up in it. 'Do you feel warmer now?' they called.

The sheet had been a rather large one and they couldn't actually see Barnaby any more. 'I feel warmer,' came the muffled reply, 'but I can't see where I'm going.' And he staggered across the room, trying not to trip over his feet.

Hearing all the muffled voices, Little Bear came trotting in through the door. He shrieked when he saw a lumpy, flapping sheet staggering across the room towards him. 'A ghost, a ghost!' he cried, and rushed to hide behind Teddy George.

'No, it's all right,' called the ghost. 'It's only me, Barnaby. I'm trying to wrap up to keep warm. I got wet in the garden.'

'Why don't you just jump up and down,' said Little Bear. 'But not dressed up as a ghost,' he added.

'All right,' said Barnaby, throwing off the sheet and jumping up and down. 'You're right. I am getting warmer, but I can't keep doing this 'til my fur's dry.'

'No,' said Teddy George, 'you can't. You're

making the plates rattle. I tell you what, I saw a hot-water bottle at the back of this cupboard one day; I could fill it with warm water from the tap. That will warm you up.' Teddy George rummaged about and found the old hot-water bottle. He took it to the tap and filled it with warm water. 'There,' he said to Barnaby, 'feel that.'

A happy smile spread across Barnaby's face as he hugged the warm hot-water bottle close to his fur. 'Oh, it's lovely,' he said. 'Thank you, Teddy George.'

Then the smile slowly left his face. 'George,' he said, slowly and thoughtfully, 'I think I know why nobody uses this hot-water bottle any more. It leaks.' He carefully laid the hot-water bottle on the ground and looked down at his fur. It was wetter than ever. Warm and wet this time.

'Oh no,' chorused the others.

'Newspaper,' said George, 'that's what we need.'

Dog rushed off and returned with the newspaper.

'Now,' said George, opening up the newspaper, 'you lie on that, Barnaby, and we'll roll you up in it. Newspaper keeps you warm and dry.'

With the help of the others, Teddy George rolled Barnaby up in the newspaper until he looked like a sausage roll.

Jane Hissey

'Now what?' said Barnaby, with only his head sticking out of the newspaper roll.

'Now we wait,' said Teddy George, sitting down.

'You can't leave me like this,' wailed Barnaby.

'We'll let you out when you're dry,' said Dog.

'But I want to get out now,' said Barnaby, rolling around the floor like a cross rolling pin. He tripped Little Bear up and then Dog, and then they all bumped into George. Soon, there was a great heap of toys in the middle of the floor. Barnaby wriggled out of the newspaper and out from under the heap. He looked at Dog with his feet in the air and George with Little Bear sitting on his middle and he began to laugh. He laughed and laughed. 'Do you know,' he said, 'all that rolling around has completely dried my fur and laughing is a wonderful way to warm up. I think I shall know what to do now if I ever get left out in the rain again.'

KATIE CAMEL AND THE DESERT PARTY

Katie Camel was miserable. Everyone had tried to cheer her up but she still seemed miserable. Little Bear had spent nearly a whole morning standing on his head, trying to make her laugh. Bramwell Brown had gone through his entire collection of jokes and Old Bear had made her breakfast in bed.

'Why are you so miserable?' asked Little Bear, at last, when he had stopped standing on his head.

'I feel lonely,' said Katie, as she nibbled sadly at a piece of Old Bear's toast. 'I had a lovely dream last night. I dreamt that I was in the desert all night. The sky was full of stars and I was playing in the sand with lots of other camels. And then I woke up,' she added sadly, 'and I found I wasn't in the desert, I was here, and it's very disappointing when one minute you're in the desert and the next, you're not. And one minute, there are lots of camels and the next, there aren't.'

'Yes,' said Little Bear, 'I expect it is. Never mind, you've got us.'

'Umm,' said Katie, doubtfully, 'but you're not much like camels, are you?'

'Er, I suppose not,' said Little Bear.

Little Bear left Katie staring sadly at a picture of a palm tree she had found in a book, and went to tell the others why she was so miserable.

'Oh dear,' said Old Bear. 'But don't worry, Little Bear, I think I have an idea.' He gathered all the toys together and whispered his plan. Soon, the whole playroom was a hive of activity. One group of toys seemed to be painting something big, and another group had needles and thread and were sewing pieces of material.

Bramwell Brown had gone out to the garden on some secret errand. Later on, when Old Bear said everything was ready, they all went to collect Katie. Katie had been so busy being miserable, that she hadn't noticed anything going on at all.

'Now Katie, we have a surprise for you,' said Old Bear, 'but we don't want you to see it until

we get you there, so I'm going to blindfold you.'
Carefully, he pulled a woolly hat down over Katie's
eyes so she couldn't see where she was going.
Then, he led her down the stairs and out into the
garden. Once there, he said, 'All right, you can
look now,' and he pulled off the woolly hat.

They were standing on the edge of the sandpit,
but oh, how different it looked! All around the
edge were cardboard cut-out palm trees that the
toys had carefully painted to look like real ones.
The sand had been raked smooth to look like the
desert and all the toys were dressed up as camels.
Some had proper camel suits on that they'd made
and others had put on coats and jumpers and had
ping-pong balls inside their jumpers to look like
humps. Some had one hump, because they were
dromedaries, some had two humps, and one rather
forgetful little teddy had three humps because he'd
lost count.

'It's a desert party,' said Old Bear, 'and you are
the very special guest, Katie.'

Katie stared in amazement at the sandpit desert
and all the teddy-bear camels and then she began
to laugh, and soon she was rolling about in the
sand laughing. 'Oh, Old Bear,' she said, when
she could find the breath to speak, 'this really has
cheered me up. How could I mind about a dream

now. All my friends are real and they make wonderful camels.'

And that night, everyone was very late to bed. They were all out in the sandpit dancing and singing by the light of the moon and the stars. Katie Camel still sometimes dreams about playing with the camels in the desert, but now the dream doesn't make her miserable. It reminds her of the surprise desert party and all her very kind friends.

THE BUNNY DANCER

Lizzie Long-ears loves to dance
With music or without it,
And if she ever gets a chance
She'll tell you all about it;
She'll mention that she leaps and lands
On just one toe and stays there
(She balances so perfectly
She might spend several days there!)
She pirouettes and hops and jumps,
And if you've ever seen her
You'll know without a doubt that
She's a bunny ballerina.

THERE WERE FOUR IN THE BED

Old bear woke with a bump when something hit him on the head. 'Don't do that,' he said, crossly, and then opened his eyes and found he was talking to the floor. 'Well, I wonder how I got down here,' he muttered, rubbing his head with his paw.

'You fell out of bed,' said a voice from above him.

Looking up, he saw a row of faces staring down at him:

Bramwell Brown the bear, Lucy the rabbit, and Duck.

'If you ask me,' said Duck, 'there are too many toys in this bed. It's overcrowded.'

'Well, it isn't too bad now,' said Lucy, 'not now that Old Bear has gone.'

'But I haven't gone!' said Old Bear.

'You look as though you have,' said Lucy, hanging dangerously over the side to see how far down Old Bear was.

'Well, I didn't mean to go,' said Old Bear. 'It just happened.'

'If a few more people happen to go,' said Duck, thoughtfully, 'the others would be able to spread out.'

'Are you hurt?' asked Bramwell Brown.

'Well, I did bump my head,' said Old Bear, glad that someone cared.

Bramwell Brown climbed down and bandaged his old friend's head with a handkerchief. 'Is that better?' he asked, kindly.

'Yes, thank you,' said Old Bear. 'You know, perhaps it is true that the bed is too crowded; I think I'll try and find somewhere else to sleep.'

'We could all look for somewhere else,' said Bramwell. 'It would be nice to have a change.'

The others climbed down too, and all four of

them set off to look for a new bed. The first place they found was an open drawer. 'This looks really good,' said Lucy Rabbit, climbing in. 'It's full of socks.'

'They're nice and soft,' said Bramwell Brown. 'I could sleep in here very comfortably.'

'And what would happen if someone shut the drawer?' asked Duck.

'Oh dear, I hadn't thought of that,' said Lucy, wriggling out of the drawer as fast as she could. 'I wouldn't want to be stuck in there forever.'

'No, drawers are not a good idea,' said Old Bear.

Bramwell Brown found a large fruit basket, next. 'I think this would be good,' he said, 'except that it's half full of fruit.'

'Oh, we could easily eat that,' said Lucy, who was always hungry, and she began to munch a large apple. Some hours later, the fruit basket was empty. Well, it was empty of fruit. Instead, four rather full toys sat in it where the fruit had been.

'It's big enough,' said Old Bear.

'But it's not very comfortable,' added Duck.

'We could come and sit in it for a change,' said Bramwell Brown, 'perhaps when we're hungry. But I don't think we could sleep here.'

'I'm so full, I could sleep anywhere,' said Lucy.

But the others dragged her out of the basket and continued to search. Lucy was soon busy pulling the cushions off all the chairs and piling them in a great heap on the floor. 'Come on, everyone,' she called from the top. 'Try it out.'

The cushions were so bouncy it made them hard to climb up but, eventually, they were all balanced on the top.

But the cushions wouldn't stay still, and soon Old Bear found himself on the floor once more.

'Oh my poor head,' he said, rubbing his bandage. 'I'm sure I keep bumping my head just because it's already been bumped. I'm going to take off my bandage.'

'We could use that handkerchief,' said Lucy, 'it would make a hammock.'

Lucy Rabbit and Bramwell Brown put the hanky hammock up between two chair legs. Old Bear decided he'd never get into a hammock, especially with someone else, and he set off for the kitchen. He'd remembered he'd seen a very comfortable looking basket there which was lined with straw and used to keep eggs in. It could be just the thing. When he arrived in the kitchen, he climbed up and settled himself in the straw like a rather

strange chicken. What luxury, he thought. If there hadn't been five eggs in the basket, there might even have been room for him to lie down. But there were five eggs, and he wasn't a chicken, so he couldn't sit on the eggs. His paws seemed to get in the way. And just as he was climbing out of the egg basket, he heard a crash. 'Oh no! What's happened now,' he said, rushing back to the other room. And there he found his friends – under the handkerchief hammock.

'It wasn't strong enough for all of us,' said Lucy. 'We fell out.'

'Do you know, I think our bed was the safest place, after all,' said Old Bear, 'but I've had an idea how we can have more room.'

And that night, if you'd peeped into their room, you would have seen Duck, Lucy Rabbit and Bramwell Brown tucked up in their usual place in bed. But down at the other end of the bed, tucked in the other way round, so his paws met theirs in the middle, was Old Bear. He had the whole end of the bed to himself and he looked very comfortable and very safe.

FLOSSIE AND GINGER AT THE SEASIDE

It was a hot summer's day and Ginger and Flossie, the two teddy bears, were on holiday at the seaside with the children. They'd all been playing hide and seek in the towels and rolling down sand hills, but now the children were going into the sea for a swim. 'You guard our buckets and spades,' they said to the bears, 'we'll be back later to build sand castles.' And with that, they skipped over the wet sand and into the waves.

'I wish we could swim,' said Ginger. 'I'm so hot under all my fur.'

'Perhaps we could cool down in the sand,' said Flossie. 'Let's build a sand castle big enough to get inside.'

The two bears set to work at once. They dug and dug. They filled the bucket over and over again to build tower upon tower. Then, while Ginger worked at the castle, Flossie dug a deep moat round it and joined it to the sea with a long canal. It filled up with water every time a wave

came in and the whole thing looked just like a real castle. Flossie and Ginger put four towers on the four corners and then made the towers look like four teddy bears with pebbles for eyes and noses and shells for ears.

'We'll call our castle "Teddy Towers",' they said, and wrote it in the sand.

'Phew, I'm really hot now,' said Flossie.

'The castle is nearly big enough to get into,' said Ginger, 'just one more spadeful.' But as Ginger pushed his spade in for the last time, it hit something hard. With his paws, he dug down to see what it was and came up with a ten-pence piece.

'Oh whoopee!' cried Flossie. 'We can go and buy ice creams now – I'm boiling.'

'That's a very good idea,' said Ginger. 'I'll finish this off while you go to the ice-cream man.'

Flossie marched happily up the beach, carrying the ten-pence piece. She found the ice-cream man standing by the heap of deck chairs. She knew it was the ice-cream man because he had a sign saying: NICE COLD ICE CREAMS – 10p each. Flossie looked at the money in her paw – it was ten pence – that meant she could only buy one ice cream with her money. Oh dear! One ice cream would never be enough to cool down two hot bears. Still, it had to be better than no ice cream. So she marched over and offered her money.

She arrived back at Teddy Towers, carefully carrying the precious ice cream, and explained to Ginger that ice creams were ten pence each. They were just about to decide who would have the first lick when a man and a woman came over to them. 'Excuse me,' they said, 'we have just come to tell you that you have won the "best sand castle on the beach" competition.

Flossie and Ginger stared in amazement. They hadn't even known there was a competition. 'Thank you,' they said, 'how exciting!'

'And your prize', said the woman, 'will be an ice cream each for every day of your holiday. Here is today's prize.' And she handed Flossie two more ice-cream cones.

'Goodness!' laughed the bears when the people had gone. 'A little while ago we had no ice creams, and now we've got three. What shall we do?'

'Well, I know what I'm going to do,' said Flossie, and she sat down in front of Teddy Towers to enjoy her prize.

And I think they were so hot they managed all three ice creams, don't you?

HENRY ISAIAH

Henry Isaiah was a bear. He was called Henry Isaiah because one eye was higher than the other one. He had been called Henry Isaiah for as long as he could remember, and for as long as he could remember he had wished he was called something else.

'Do you think I ever had another name?' he asked his friend Rags one day.

'Well, I suppose if your eyes were straight when you were new, Isaiah would have been a silly name,' said Rags. 'Perhaps you were called something else then.'

'I wish I had a nice short name like yours,' said Henry Isaiah.

'You wouldn't want to be called Rags would you?' said Rags. 'I think it means I look like a rag-bag with bits of material mending my paws. I was a smart new bear once, but I've been hugged until I'm threadbare. I can't always have been called Rags, but nobody remembers the name I had when I was new. If you want to find someone who will remember your old name,

123

you'd better ask Furless Fred. He's even older than me and he remembers us all when we were new.'

Henry Isaiah found Furless Fred sitting in the garden amongst the flowers.

'Furless,' said Henry Isaiah, 'was I always called Henry Isaiah?'

'I think so,' said Furless. 'Your eyes were like that when you were new – one up and one down.'

'But it's such a silly name,' said Henry Isaiah.

'Not as silly as Furless Fred,' said Furless Fred. 'I was just called Fred once, but I've been left in the garden so many times now all my fur is worn off and everyone calls me Furless.'

'Well, if I never had a better name,' said Henry Isaiah, 'then I'll invent one. I shall call myself something smart and distinguished. I'll call myself James.'

'That's all right,' said Furless Fred, 'you can call yourself anything you like as long as everyone knows your new name.'

'How can I tell everyone my new name?' asked Henry Isaiah, who was now called James.

'Well, we could have a new name party for you and tell all the other toys at the party.'

'That's a very good idea,' said Rags. 'I shall send out the invitations at once. If I find Dog he'll be postman and take the invitations to everyone.'

James Bear, who used to be Henry Isaiah, went back happily to wait for his party invitation. He snuggled down under a blanket and dreamed of party hats and jellies and everyone calling him James. It would be the best party ever. Rags and Furless Fred carefully wrote out the invitations to everyone. They remembered to put James and not Henry Isaiah on Henry Isaiah's invitation and they gave them all to Dog to deliver. The next day everyone started arriving for the party. Nobody knew why they were having the party and some had brought presents in case it was anyone's birthday.

'It's a surprise party,' said Rags. 'Somebody wants to tell you something and he's going to tell you at the party.'

'Ooh,' said the toys, 'it sounds exciting.' Rabbit started to organize some games and soon everyone was having a lovely time. Rags and Furless Fred waited for James, who had been Henry Isaiah, to arrive, but he didn't. Soon everyone was hungry.

'Well, you'd better start on the food,' said Rags, peering out of the door to try and catch sight of the missing guest. Where could he be? They'd sent him an invitation with the time and the place of the party. When everyone had finished their party food and begun to go home, Rags called Dog over. 'Dog,' he said, 'you did deliver all the invitations didn't you?'

'Of course I did,' said Dog, 'all except one.'

'Which one?' said Furless Fred and Rags at the same time.

'This one,' said Dog, producing a crumpled piece of paper he was carrying, 'it's addressed to someone called James. I asked everyone but nobody knew who that was.'

'Oh, no,' cried Rags, 'we forgot to tell Dog and now James, who was Henry Isaiah, has missed his own naming party.'

Rushing out of the room, they bumped straight into James. He was standing miserably, watching everyone going home from the party carrying balloons and pieces of cake. 'Was that my party?' he asked, sadly.

'Oh, James,' said Rags, 'I'm so sorry.' And he explained how Dog did not know where to take the invitation.

'Did I miss the games?' asked James.

'I'm afraid so,' said Rags.

'And the food?' asked James.

'And the food,' said Furless Fred.

'All because I changed my name?' asked the very miserable bear.

'I'm afraid so,' said the others.

'Perhaps changing one's name is a bit risky,' said James, who was Henry Isaiah. 'I wouldn't want to miss any more parties, do you think perhaps I ought to change my name back to Henry Isaiah?'

'Perhaps that would be best,' said Rags, 'it's a very nice name you know, a very memorable name.'

'Yes, perhaps it isn't so bad,' said Henry Isaiah, who had briefly been James. 'Did you save me a balloon?'

'Of course we did,' said Furless Fred and Rags. 'Shall we write your name on it?' And they did. And Henry Isaiah proudly walked home with a big red balloon with 'Henry Isaiah' written on it.

Henry Isaiah is the right sort of name to have on a balloon, he thought to himself. It's nice and long and goes all the way round to the other side. It's twice as long as James.

THE CIRCUS

There had been a birthday party at the house where Old Bear and his friends lived. The big round table in the dining room had a big round cloth on it, and there, on top of the table was all the food that hadn't been eaten at the party. And there had been *so* much food, that an awful lot was still there. 'Just look at it all,' said Little Bear, 'we could have a feast if we could reach it.'

Unfortunately, all the chairs had been taken to another room for a game of musical chairs and there wasn't one to climb on to reach the food. Little Bear popped his head under the tablecloth to see whether there was a way up from the inside and squeaked with excitement. 'Look everyone!' he shouted, 'it's like a circus tent in here – a big top!'

The others popped their heads in too and soon all the toys had joined them. It really was like a huge, round tent. 'We could have a circus instead of a party,' said Bruno the big brown bear.

'How *do* you have a circus?' asked Little Bear.

'Well, everyone goes into the big top, or under the table in our case, and some people watch and some people do tricks.'

'And the people who watch have to clap and cheer,' added Sailor.

'It's a lovely idea,' said Rabbit. 'I could do jumping.'

'Jumping isn't a trick,' said Little Bear.

'It is if you jump very high or over something,' said Rabbit.

'Over what?' asked Little Bear.

'Rabbit could jump over me if he liked,' said Zebra, 'that would be a trick.'

Rabbit and Zebra practised their trick lots of times while the other toys discussed what they could do in the circus.

'I think I could juggle,' said Little Bear, 'almost.'

'And I could walk a tightrope,' said Sailor. 'If I could borrow your trousers,' he said to Little Bear, 'I could dress up as a clown, too.'

'That would be good,' said Bruno, 'but we need lots more acts. What can you do, Camel?'

'I don't know,' said Camel. 'If I ran round and round the big top, could someone balance on one of my humps?'

'We could try,' said Bruno.

Everyone had a go at standing up on Camel's humps. But nobody could do it except Rabbit, even when Camel stood still. Rabbit could stand on one leg, waggle his ears, hop up and down and even jump up in the air, whilst balancing on one of Camel's humps. Everyone was most impressed.

'You're good at tricks, aren't you,' said Bruno. 'What else can you do?'

There was no doubt about it, Rabbit was going to be the star of the show. By the time he'd shown them how he could hang from things just by his feet, jump through a hoop, and juggle with three bean bags, the others all wanted to be the audience.

'We'll never be as good as Rabbit,' they all said.

'It doesn't matter,' said Bruno. 'Circuses are just meant to be fun. We don't really have to be good at everything.'

'Let's begin,' said Old Bear. He lifted a corner of the tablecloth to make an entrance, and all the toys marched in under the table. It was very exciting.

'I've never been to a circus, before,' said Duck.

'I don't think any of us have,' said Bruno, taking his place as ringmaster in the middle of the ring.

The toys all sat around the edge and Rabbit and Zebra stepped forward to do the first trick. Everyone clapped and cheered as Rabbit ran across the ring and leaped over Zebra's back. He landed on Old Bear's lap. But the other toys thought that was part of the trick. He did it a few more times until Bruno stopped him, and then Sailor came into the ring.

Sailor tied a skipping rope between two table legs and the toys watched excitedly as he carefully walked along the rope. He did fall off once, but he landed on one of the other toys, so he didn't hurt himself. Swinging himself back up again, he tried juggling this time while balancing.

'Well done!' called Old Bear. 'That's wonderful.'

It was Dog's turn next. He strolled into the ring balancing one of his rubber bones on his nose. 'I was going to balance two,' he said, 'but I couldn't remember where I buried the other one.'

Everyone clapped hard and he bowed and left the ring. And as he left, Camel came in. She trotted around the ring until Rabbit appeared and then, with Rabbit perched on a hump, she began to run really fast. Rabbit bounced about, standing first on one leg and then on the other. 'What shall I do for my next trick?' he called.

'Hop,' shouted one of the toys.

Camel thought they shouted, 'Stop,' and stopped so suddenly that Rabbit sailed through the air and hit the tablecloth. Grabbing wildly at it, he clung on and then, quite slowly, pulled the whole thing down. Plates of food landed all around the table and, in a second,

136

the circus tent had vanished. Rabbit, unhurt, wriggled out from under the cloth and looked at the food lying all around them. 'Oh dear,' he said, 'did I do that?'

'Never mind, Rabbit,' said Old Bear. 'We may have lost our circus but we found the feast. We never thought about pulling down the tablecloth to get all the food. Have a bun.'

'Oooh, I could juggle with these buns,' said Rabbit.

'Let's just eat them, shall we?' suggested Old Bear and, sitting under the table to eat, they enjoyed the food almost as much as they'd enjoyed the circus.